To Kate, who finds friendship
in the most extraordinary kind of places.

Neal Porter Books

Text and illustrations copyright © 2022 by Suzanne Kaufman

All Rights Reserved

HOLIDAY HOUSE is registered in the U.S. Patent and Trademark Office.

Printed and bound in April 2022 at Toppan Leefung, DongGuan, China.

The artwork for this book was created with ink and opaque watercolor.

Book design by Jennifer Browne

www.holidayhouse.com

First Edition

10   9   8   7   6   5   4   3   2   1

Library of Congress Cataloging-in-Publication Data

Names: Kaufman, Suzanne, author, illustrator.

Title: A friend for Ghost / Suzanne Kaufman.

Description: First edition. | New York City : Holiday House, [2022] | "A
   Neal Porter Book." | Audience: Ages 4 to 8 | Audience: Grades K–1 |
   Summary: "A lonely ghost finds a friend in a bright red balloon"—
   Provided by publisher.

Identifiers: LCCN 2021038966 | ISBN 9780823448524 (hardcover)

Subjects: LCSH: Loneliness—Juvenile fiction. | Friendship—Juvenile
   fiction. | CYAC: Ghosts—Fiction. | Loneliness—Fiction. |
   Friendship—Fiction. | LCGFT: Picture books.

Classification: LCC PZ7.1.K378 Fr 2022 | DDC 813.6 [E]—dc23/eng/20211012

LC record available at https://lccn.loc.gov/2021038966

ISBN 978-0-8234-4852-4   (hardcover)

Suzanne Kaufman

a friend
for
ghost

NEAL PORTER BOOKS

HOLIDAY HOUSE / NEW YORK

Above a noisy family,
on a crowded street,
in the big city,
in a dark lonely attic,
lived Ghost.

Most of the time
no one noticed Ghost.

But not all
of the time.

Ghost drifted . . .

and lingered . . .

Always alone
in the crowd.

Until one day. . .

something drifted Ghost's way.

Could it be . . . a friend?

They played everywhere

and they shared everything . . .

. . . even the
scary stuff.

Anything Ghost wanted to do,
the friend was sure to follow.

"It's your turn to hide," said Ghost.

"WAIT!"

Ghost searched
high and low . . .

. . . and everywhere inbetween.

But nothing seemed to work.
Ghost's friend had vanished.

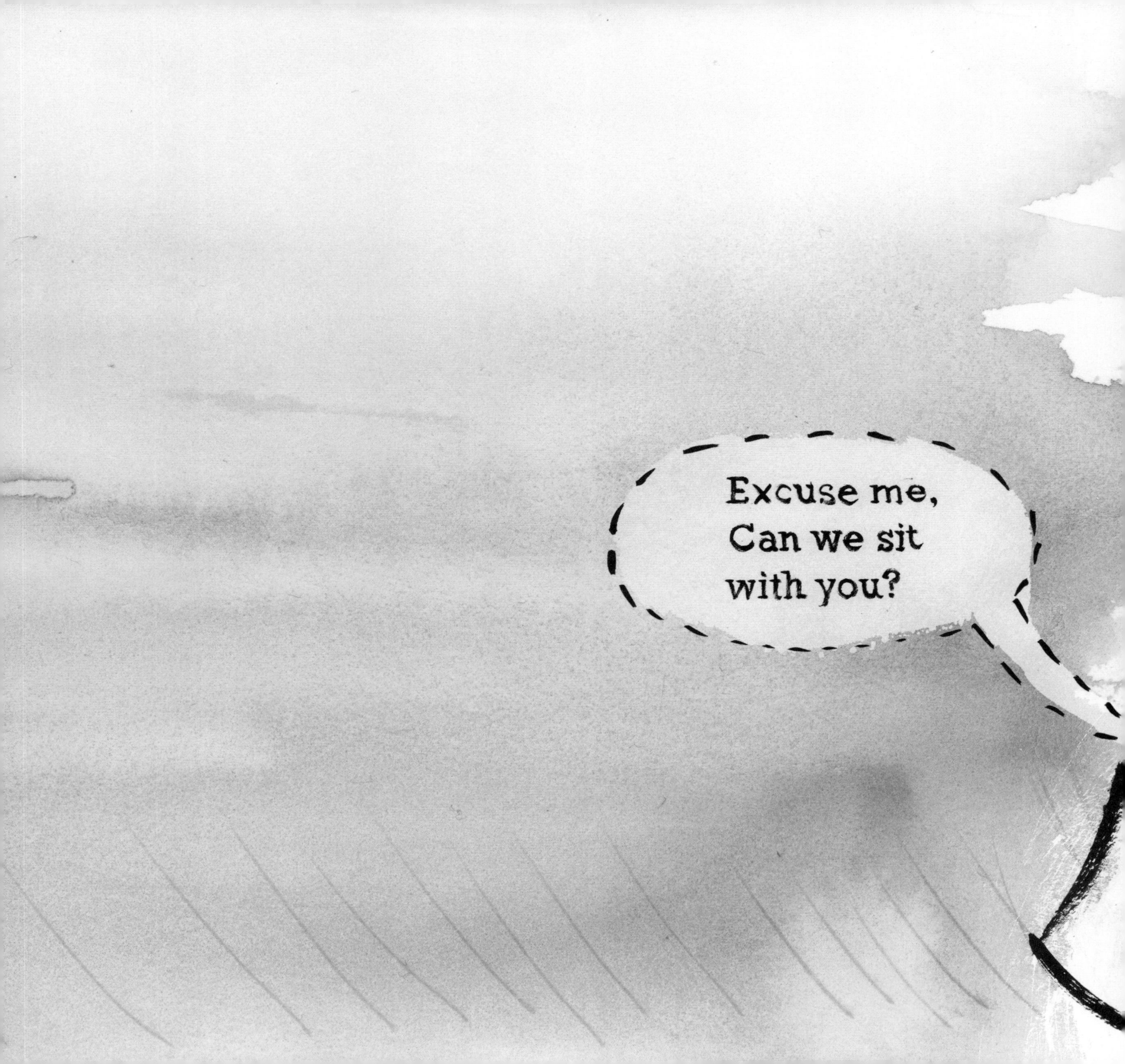
Excuse me, Can we sit with you?

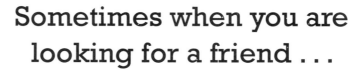
Sometimes when you are looking for a friend . . .

A friend finds you.